Very Short
Stories

Very Short Stories

300 Bite-Size Works of Fiction

Sean Hill

Interior illustrations by Evan Wondolowski

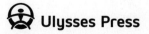 Ulysses Press

Published in the United States by
ULYSSES PRESS
P.O. Box 3440
Berkeley, CA 94703
www.ulyssespress.com

ISBN 978-1-61243-016-4
Library of Congress Control Number 2011934784

Acquisitions Editor: Kelly Reed
Managing Editor: Claire Chun
Editor: Melissa Stein
Proofreader: Lauren Harrison
Design and layout: what!design @ whatweb.com
Front cover illustration: © Chloë Marr-Fuller
Back cover illustrations: © Evan Wondolowski

Printed in the United States by Bang Printing

10 9 8 7 6 5 4 3 2 1

Dedication

For my monkeys. When you're older you can read this.

Each word I write drops a little more of me onto the page. In time, I will be the book, the book will be me, and the story will be told.

Table of Contents

Introduction

This book started as an experiment on Twitter. I've heard people talk about writer's block but never really believed in it. I wanted to find out for myself if I could run out of ideas. If I wrote down all of the stories I could think of, would more ideas arrive to fill the void?

So far the answer has been yes.

I've written over 700 of these bite-size stories so far, and more arrive in my mind each time I sit down to write. There have been a few times when the next story did not turn up on schedule, and I wondered if I was done. At these moments, I had a couple of tricks I used to keep the ideas flowing.

Trick #1 — I asked my followers on Twitter to send me a noun for inspiration. The nouns that inspired me I used in a story. I like this trick a lot. I learned it teaching and performing improv comedy, where we often ask the audience for a suggestion to inspire a scene. My favorite thing about this trick is that it makes the writing a collaborative process.

There are so many stories in this collection that I would never have written if I had not received a noun from a reader. I've found that by collaborating creatively with others, we can go some place together that neither one of us would have gone alone.

There is an important part to this trick. I do not use suggestions that do not inspire me. It's the same when I perform improv comedy. I ask the audience for several suggestions and look at the faces of my fellow performers to see when a suggestion inspires them. It's easy to tell—their faces light up when they are inspired. When I see that, I know we're ready to create.

Trick #2 — Be willing to write a bad story. I think this is the place that most people experience what they call writer's block. It has to do with judging the results as we're creating them. If you judge as you create, then you start to edit yourself before you have a chance to express the thoughts. This can lead to creative paralysis. My improv comedy training has freed me from this burden. I know that sometimes the work I produce will be good, sometimes it will be so-so, and on some occasions the special magic will happen and it will be spectacular. So instead of wondering whether the current story will be any good, I just keep writing. Sometimes when a story is done and I don't feel it's one of my best, I send it out into the world anyway. This reminds me not to be attached to the results, keeps me humble, and makes way for the next story to arrive.

The most unexpected part of this book has been the wonderful response I've gotten from the followers of my stories on Twitter. Every day, people I don't know, from all over the world, write to me to say how much they enjoy the stories I've written. Strangers have been wonderfully kind and supportive. They continue to send me nouns to inspire more stories. It's the interacting and collaborating with readers that made the process of creating this book so wonderfully joyous.

Join the conversation and collaborate on more stories:
Twitter.com/veryshortstory
Facebook.com/veryshortstory

—Sean Hill

Chapter 1:

Relationships

I wrote "I love you" a thousand times on the walls, but you were too deep in a romance novel to notice I wanted to be more than roommates.

Chris likes cougars. They're experienced. They're sexy. The things they could do together. If only he could catch one. Chris is 85.

I put myself on the curb and waited
for the trash truck to collect me.
Hoping to find you. Didn't mean to
call you trashy.

Suzy wasn't sure why she liked Trey.
He didn't have much money and wasn't
good looking. Maybe the fact he loved
her counted for something.

I never had much luck with women till that day in the lab. Then things changed. Now, they can't get enough of me. Seems invisible is sexy.

Called my dad to let him know my wife, Janice, was gone. "What happened?" asked my dad. "My fault," I said, "forgot to lock the door."

Marrying a robot wife was the answer to my loneliness, until I woke up to an empty bed and found her cuddling the refrigerator.

I met Mary in the grocery store. She smiled at me and I fell in love instantly, missing the red flag that she was wearing only one shoe.

For Walt, there were two kinds of women: those who liked him and those who didn't. He only liked those who didn't, sensing their good taste.

He married her, saying how special she was. Then at her happiest moment, he touched her, turning her to stone, so her feeling would last.

I strapped on my goggles and jumped into the flames. I loved Mirabel. Dammed if I'd let the Devil have her because she had impure thoughts.

I put the poison in the cup and we sat
down to tea. My wife, Hilda, chattered
on, not noticing I'd expired, finally
finding peace and quiet.

Met Alysa on the beach. Took her to
my car, dried her off. When legs did
not magically appear, I lost interest,
dropped her at the aquarium.

Mona softly opened the door and turned on her flashlight. He was sleeping. She couldn't get her dignity back, but she could get her money.

Would she still love me? I rang the doorbell. It opened. She was still beautiful. "Pookie!" she said, just like she did 50 years ago.

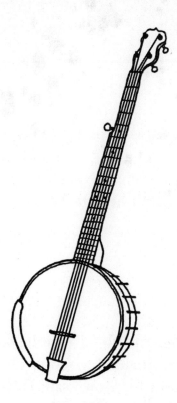

Met Ellie at a club, fell in love, and asked her to move in. The next day she arrived at my house holding a banjo. I knew we were doomed.

Math has always been my favorite subject. I get along with numbers. They make sense. Numbers don't lie. Why couldn't he be a number?

Climbing into the dirigible, we embraced, thrilled to elope. Everything was perfect. "Uh-oh," said David, "One of us has to cast off."

"Do you love me, Phillip?" asked Priscilla. "That's a silly question," he replied, still looking at his paper. "I thought so," she said.

Clowning was Daryl's profession, cooking was his passion. Stella thought he was perfect. She liked to laugh and never learned to cook.

Dana got in the cab wanting to get home. Bad blind date. Alone. Feeling desperate. "You want to get a drink?" she asked the cabbie.

Johnny worked up his nerve. "You want to go on a date?" "I don't think that is a good idea," said Ms. Brackle, his 5th grade teacher.

The catapult launched Tom toward Kim's window. He crashed through with the banner proclaiming his love. She, however, was at the pool.

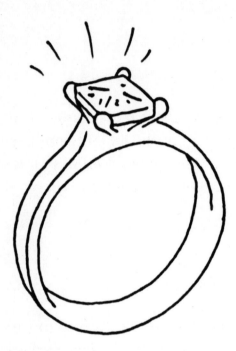

Alex bought Sharon a ring for
Valentine's Day, which she sold to
buy the gun that stopped him from
loving her.

Jim and Stella shredded their relationship in the lobby. Screaming about never seeing each other but joined by the last available room.

Jack told his girlfriend problems to his rock collection. They were old and wise, knowing just to listen, not tell him what to do.

Darla's beauty was staggering…
literally. When men saw her, they
staggered and fell down. Lonely, she
resorted to dating blind men.

David liked ants, the only pet his
parents had approved of. He designed
his house like an ant colony but still
searched for his queen.

Read your diary, discovered your secret. I thought I loved you, but now I'm not sure. Don't know what to do, you look so human.

Justin probed Mary's cerebral cortex, removing the unwanted thoughts. No longer would she think of sweets, now she would crave him.

Sheila liked Ken in the same way she liked a Filet-O-Fish sandwich when she was thinking of lobster. He was right here, right now.

After swimming, Tom walked on the beach, unable to find his hotel. Rita, sure he'd left her, spent their wedding night with the bellboy.

The date went poorly. Wendal and Marge discovered nothing in common and didn't know what to talk about when they woke up in the morning.

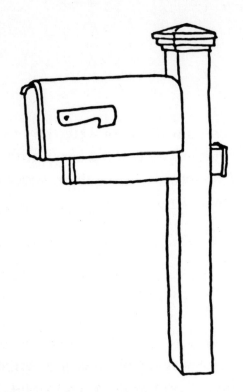

Silas camped by the mailbox, waiting on his pen pal's letter. In love with Marie, he was destroyed to learn she was an old man in prison.

I wore the flip-flops everywhere.
When they wore out, I carried the
pieces. Beautiful Rita said she'd be
back for them. I was waiting.

I used my second wish to undo the
first. Your body sprang back to life.
The third wish I'm keeping, in case
you get out of line again.

He loved her through her multitude of boyfriends, hoping she'd come to her senses and love him. Finally he settled for her sister.

Tony was sure that Eunice wanted him. When he proposed, she didn't know how to explain that he was her imaginary friend.

Some people get things bronzed, I had my first wife encased in gold. I really liked her. I won't let one indiscretion tarnish her memory.

Kim walked down the aisle. Suddenly she saw herself burst into the room. "Stop! Don't marry Phil! You'll learn to love yourself!"

Outside the window, Mark stood in the moonlight, serenading Vicky. Her heart remained closed, unmoved by the sounds of his tuba.

Tired of being wanted for her looks, Kim shaved her head before the blind date. Ted dressed like a tramp, hiding his wealth. Both ran.

Walter loved Jillian, the librarian. He longed to sort her stacks, turn her pages, but they were shelved apart, classics and new releases.

It worked. Clara had finally gotten Donald to marry her. Happy at last. Somehow she would hide the fact there was no inheritance.

The postcard arrived in May. "Sorry" was all it said. At least, I knew now, Bridget was alive. Wish she had shown up for our honeymoon.

Years later, sitting along in his mansion, with no one to hold him, it finally hit him. "This is what she meant."

After our date, we went home and found your place had been robbed. It made me feel bad about all the times I thought about robbing you.

Dear Chocolate Cake, Last night was so special. I've never been kissed like that. You're the one. Hope you feel the same. Check yes or no.

Seven more days of school. Seven more chances for him to notice her. Lilly's outfits got sexier each day. Brian and his guide dog never noticed.

I fell in love with Georgette the first time she whispered in my ear. Her body was all woman, but she had the mind of a truck driver.

Karen slipped out of John's bed and made the long walk home. At first it was just for fun, but when love arrived it was time for her to go.

Darla snuggled Rick on the plane, headed for a second honeymoon. Things had changed since her coma. She'd forgotten all about his affairs.

Leeann's words crushed Brian's heart like a sledgehammer. Their relationship was ruined. How could she have said it? "Who is Spock?"

First date with HotGinger142 tonight. I hid my soul under the bed. Things I do with people I meet online, I don't want my soul to see.

Marla began to fidget behind the desk. "Well?" said Dave, still holding out the ring. Marla raised her hand showing the ring from Bob.

Roy found her scarf on the sidewalk.
Left for him? An invitation? He ran to
look for her. Relieved, Sara snuck back
into the party.

Kim refused to walk down the runway
in the swimsuit. I yelled through
the megaphone, "You are not fat!" to
overcome the voices in her head.

Ted eased the boat out of the slip. Betty was impressed. She hoped he maneuvered that well in bed, but even if he didn't, he had a boat.

I could tell by her fur she wasn't from around here. We chitchatted. I put on the moves. We went to my place. In spring, we had cubs.

Ty softly tossed a pebble at Jill's window. In return, a large rock hit him squarely in the head. He would take that as a "no."

"Do you ever wish you had married someone else?" asked Gina. Albert's brain went into overdrive seeking the correct answer. "No?"

"You are a liar!" said Christy. "Only about that," said John. "That still makes you a liar!" "OK…I do think you're fat. That better?"

The serendipity of the situation amused Carl. He had left his wife, May, and fallen in love with June, her divorce lawyer.

You asked for flowers and I brought flowers. You asked for dancing and I danced. I asked for your love and you gave back the flowers.

4 a.m. You are awake. I am awake. We are having THE talk. In the morning I will pretend to look for work.

"You are the Holy Grail of girlfriends," said John. Erica smiled and snuggled close to enjoy the moment. His wife would be home soon.

Bill left the coffee shop disappointed.
She hadn't come. He felt rejected. Pam
waited patiently at another Starbucks
across the street.

Mindy didn't go anywhere without her cherry-flavored Chapstick. Paul resented it. He wanted to be the one caressing those lips.

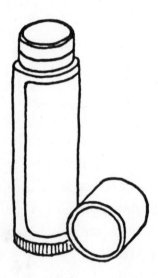

Karen lay back on the piano, inviting Kyle to have her. Unaware, he continued to discuss the nuances of Bach and how they excited him.

"I'm glad you're sleeping over," said Kent. "I feel safe with you," said Lori. He turned on his Batman night-light. Now they both felt safe.

"I need commitment," said Amy. Mark ripped off his shirt and wrote "Amy's" on his chest in permanent marker. Now, she felt safe to love him.

"Yes, I'll marry you," she said. Then I asked, "You're picking ME right, not because I'm the last man on Earth?" She bit her lip. "Ummm…."

Walter sat staring at the screen.
Melissa's IM invited him to coffee.
He paused for a moment then pushed
delete. Walter preferred tea.

Marty and Warren eased through the warehouse window. After tonight they'd be rich, then finally they'd be together. Weddings are expensive.

Chapter 2:

Family

Lyle flashed on the future, seeing his daughter and her playmate married, living in a trailer. He promptly moved her to another preschool.

The backstage pass was Arthur's chance to finally meet his dad, but after seeing the over-the-hill rocker perform, he settled for the poster.

I took the jar down from the shelf, opened it, and spoke to my father's heart, telling him I loved him…finally conversing heart-to-heart.

"Do you think they're coming back?" asked Julie. "No," I said, "They were happy driving away." My sister and I raised ourselves after that.

The other chickens looked on in horror as Vern lowered himself into the deep fryer. With Farmer gone, it was up to him to feed his family.

"Fire truck!" yelled five-year-old Billy. His mom had told him his dad was a fireman. When he got older he set fires, hoping to meet Dad.

After the meal, the men gathered around the TV to watch sports, sitting there in awkward silence when the cable went out.

The kids begged me and I gave in. A trip for three to the moon. Much more expensive than when I was a kid. We used to just imagine going.

Some parents push their kids to be sports stars. With me it's superheroes. White Donut and Double Talker, those are MY children.

"I'm an artist," said Rick. "My canvas is the childhood of my children. I color it with laughter, joy, inspiration, hoping it all gels."

The overflowing pile of laundry swallowed Marge. With her final thought, she wondered why she thought it was a good idea to have five kids.

Jack threw a piece of candy on the floor
and watched his three children fight
for it. The winner was groomed to
protect Jack as he grew old.

I looked all through my mind for
memories of you. Unable to find any,
I had to take your word for it that you
were my father.

I dated Sara, accepting her kids as my own. She disappeared after our wedding vows, leaving a note: "Thanks for watching the kids."

Zara woke up to find the severed head of a pink My Little Pony in her bed. The message was clear. She returned her brother's GI Joe.

Carl opened the oven and the chicken
leapt out, apparently not done yet. The
children sat at the table wondering
when Mom would return.

I handed Tom his birthday present. Awkward pause. "Didn't you get ME anything?" I asked. "I forgot." We're not the closest of twins.

Carlton is blind. In desperation, he had stared into the sun. He knew now, nothing would erase the image of his parents having sex.

The clock had belonged to my grandfather, given to him by the king. Now, I was giving it to my son so he too could watch his life tick by.

Momentary serenity. Sitting on the bottom of the pool, a brief vacation from the world. Soon, they will find me. My kids always do.

Jim's car was missing. A tricycle with a note was parked in its place. "Late for SAT. Borrowed car." It's difficult raising a genius.

Very Short Stories

"Happy Mother's Day!" said Zara,
"You're the best mother ever!" Smiling,
I hug her tight, feeling the spirit of my
wife close by.

Rena gave away her first child for
money. The second child, she kept. He
would make a good house cleaner and
now she could afford one.

At the movies. You hold my hand as
the actor turns into a creepy werewolf.
You start to cry. First time you've seen
your dad in makeup.

"Surrender or die!" he said, pointing
the gun at me. I panic. The five year
old pulls the trigger, hitting me in the
head with the water.

Ernie stared at the pile of papers on his desk. What to keep? What to throw away? Why did the teacher let his kid make so much art?

The coffee stained Tim's breath as he drank it. No longer in love with his wife, he used it to build a shield around himself.

Don's mother moved in unexpectedly. She tagged along everywhere. She had given him the best years of her life and now she was taking his.

Levi was very proud of his mustache. He drew a sense of power from it. Now the two of them lived alone. Lana didn't want a threesome.

"Winning is everything," my dad always said. "As long as it's fun," I told my son after a dropped pass. Wish I'd heard it as a kid.

Nana rocked in her old wooden rocking chair. "Timmy, you have always been my favorite," she said. He looked at her. "Nana, I'm Bobby."

Allen lifted the money from Nana's purse and hurried outside. He told himself she didn't need it and how else could he buy her a birthday gift?

Nancy's life felt like quicksand. No way to get out. She needed a rope or a branch or a hand. Her mother had given her an anvil.

I attached the transmitter to my daughter's skull. As I suspected, her thoughts were not all sugar and spice and everything nice.

There could be only one winner. We faced each other. He struck first, but I was quicker. It would be my child opening the last toy tomorrow.

I listened patiently for you to make a noise, but you never did. Reluctantly, I had to admit you were right, it was a bottomless pit.

I switched on my antigravity boots in an effort to escape your overbearing ways, but you fired a harpoon of guilt that prevented my ascent.

I found you in a tent on the beach and handcuffed us together while you slept, making sure you wouldn't abandon me the way you did Mom.

The fire felt good. It drove away the thoughts of you as it caressed my skin. I hoped there was no afterlife from which to remember you.

I watched you walk by in your high heels and short skirt. My friends whistled, but all I could think about was when you used to be my dad.

Brought home a talking mule to impress my family, but he was a smooth talker. He quickly turned them against me, taking my spot at the table.

Darleen asked Joyce, "Are you my mother?" "I am now, sweetie. Do you want to play a game?" Darleen chose checkers from Joyce's menu.

I watched my brothers grow up from
the woods behind our house, hoping
they would not make the same mistake
of beating our father at chess.

Chapter 3:
Life

Monday crept over Jack, killing
his mood. The weekend had been
great. He'd partied like there was no
tomorrow, but unfortunately there was.

Kevin stood outside in the rain,
wishing out loud it would last forever…
and it did. Neighbors blamed him when
they had to replace cars with boats.

Tom quietly stared at the candelabra while he ate his food. Things had changed since he was a kid. This was not the McDonald's of his youth.

Jared cried on New Year's Day. The fortune-teller said this year would be his last, and it would…although it was just a lucky guess.

Each new wrinkle was a mark of a lesson learned. The years had filled me with knowledge, but I sat alone, the young ones not seeing my value.

Offended to be sat on, the new chair bit Randy's arm. He ignited the possessed chair with a flamethrower. The store refused the return.

I enjoyed my morning coffee on the veranda, listening to the symphony of metal below, as I admired the shiny stop signs I'd acquired.

The coin dropped into the slot and that sweet feeling returned. My problems faded. I am powerful. You cannot stop me. I AM Ms. Pac-man!

David likes to record. He documents each moment of his life. Photos, video, audio. He never watches any of it. Not even when it happened.

Allen dropped the needle into the groove. Marching music played loudly. He started to feel better. Five minutes till the next patient.

Vince's magnificent hair was the source of his charm. Ladies swooned. He worked hard to preserve it, mastering the comb-over pompadour.

Thoughts of you inheriting my fortune
got me from my death bed. Money
made life easy. I never discovered who I
was. I'd save you from that.

They found Jim's body at the bottom
of the pool, under the blueberries.
An attempt at the world's record for
biggest dessert gone wrong.

Old Willie wanted to see his childhood home again. David, the nursing home orderly, freed Willie, returning him to his natural habitat.

Thought about what you said, how maybe none of this is real. Decided to re-imagine my life. Now you're prettier and make me think less.

Running late, Tom searched for
his luggage among the bags going
around. Too many looked the same.
He screamed, grabbed one, and left.

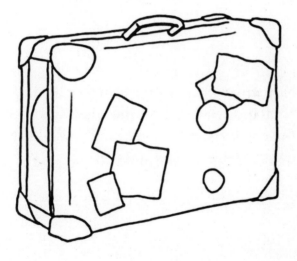

Vern put on his tap shoes. He danced, having just finished his memoir. Suddenly, he stopped, wondering if he should include the dancing.

Saw my enemy from ninth grade, Ted Nedland, walking on the road. I lunged the car forward. "Look out!" yelled my wife. No time to explain.

Wondering if I am real. Am I just a character in a story? My past seems vague, my future limited. Please, if you made me, let me know.

"God, help me," Doug cried. The sky opened up, God reached down and plucked him up. Part of the new personalized customer service plan.

Marco loved high heel shoes on women. He loved them on himself even more. It made his mother regret the time she made him wear a dress.

Tommy found his mother on the floor, her back broken. His mind rushed back to the walk home, paying no attention to where he stepped.

No one saw it coming. The students took over on the first day of school, led by the kindergartners, who weren't yet drones of the system.

Psst! It's me…I mean you, from the future. Don't worry, it works out. You'll be wrongly convicted but meet your true love in prison.

The water came and washed away everything. I wondered if God was playing with his toys the same way I played as a child by the stream.

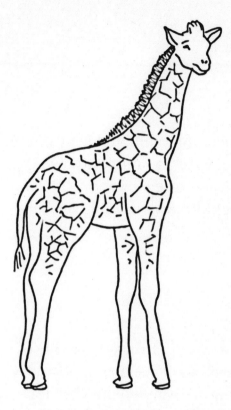

On his 50th birthday, Phil saddled a
giraffe and rode through town. His
wife waited patiently as he reclaimed
the dreams of his youth.

Alone in my cabin, hidden from the world, I ate a peanut butter–banana sandwich to celebrate my birthday and thought back to when I was king.

Barry stared at the empty side of the bed, finally realizing no one was coming to complete his life. This was it. Time to start living.

"My day is better than yours," Kevin taunted in his Facebook status update, unaware the others had already been evacuated from Earth.

There you were, walking along holding hands with our minister, Rick. Just weeks after the children and I said goodbye to your ashes.

Gerald cared for his mom's neglected plants. Grateful, a fern felt compelled to speak, "Thank you." Terrified, he got rid of the plants.

The doctors attached a younger arm to my body so I could throw the ball downfield. Now, if they could stop the hits to my 70-year-old chest.

The scar was part of Don's charm. Women would ask about it and he would tell the elaborate tale, although the truth was he fell in the shower.

My body broke down on the long journey. With no spare parts available, I discarded it and continued on my quest for enlightenment.

Opened my front door, found a baby with a note. "This is yours." Tried to remember who I'd slept with. Gotta stop drinking.

Valarie used her baby spoon from childhood to eat wherever she went. Her happiest memories were before boys, bills, and responsibilities.

Cindy shook her money maker, late at night, for tips. She dreamed of being a dentist, fixing the broken smiles that gawked at her.

"Yes, there were things called newspapers. People would buy them to read about what happened the day before." "Daddy, what's paper?"

It was you. Your kiss that injected me with this sickness. Your passionate, wet, slobbery, flu-ridden kiss. Let me return the favor.

Bert put the saxophone on the counter
and picked up the $20. In the morning,
he would be gone, before his son
missed his instrument.

Bill and Keith sped past the fires, mudslides, and earthquakes. This was LA. To get your movie deal, those were minor obstacles.

4 a.m. You are asleep. I am awake. I am trying on your clothes. In the morning, you will wake up alone with nothing to wear.

Re-shelving books, Walter found pics of Jilly, the librarian, lying nude on a huge pile of books. She'd do anything to promote reading.

It was the moment that changed Sam's life. Mary said yes to prom. It led to kissing, marriage, two kids, divorce, alimony, and loneliness.

Rex played in the wine cellar during the party. Parents embarrassed by their untalented child. He wrote his best-selling memoir there.

It had started with a three-day weekend. Julie had lounged and taken it easy. Now, the bed had her and wasn't letting go.

Megan walked inside from the rain. Disappointed it hadn't worked. None of her troubles had been washed away. She was still pregnant.

Ken sat opposite the bear on the life raft. Each eyeing the other. Soon the food would run out and somebody would get eaten.

I bought a jaguar today. Not a car, an ACTUAL jaguar. I figure it will impress women more than a car. I got a two-seat saddle for it.

After losing his job, Nigel lived
without caution. Even when the
forecast called for rain, he refused to
carry an umbrella.

Jared won the lottery. He bought
a diamond-encrusted fountain pen.
Big mistake. It inspired him to write
checks, spending all the money.

Mitch looked through the pictures in
the camera hoping to find one he liked.
Unfortunately, they were all of him.

"Never did this before," said Gina. She fumbles with the lock and opens her door. Inside I hand her the $50. She hands me the homework.

The power went out. The elevator stopped. In the dark you told me your fears and cried. The next day you fired me to keep your secrets safe.

I used to like pineapple. Don't like it
anymore. Four years. It was the only
thing that would grow on that island.

Marlene's artichoke dip was the talk of the town. In the small town of Bransford, she was the cutting edge of culture.

Jeremy stared at his picture above the mantelpiece. The picture mocked him. It was fit and trim. It had hair. It still had potential.

Nan rode the stallion toward the fence, leaping when they got close. The perfect escape if the horse had leapt with her.

Paul crunched all of the bags of potato chips on the store shelves. If he couldn't eat them on his diet, neither would anyone else.

I swept the fear from the dark corners
of my mind & stepped outside. There
you were, standing in the sunshine of
life, waiting to play with me.

Officer Ryan just missed the ledge
as he leapt across buildings while
pursuing the suspect. Thinking as he
fell, "I hate Mondays."

Chapter 4:

Sex

I answered the ad for "slave wanted," ready for some adventure. That's when I met Sheila, who was celibate but needed a lot of chores done.

"Again!" said Rosa. "Are you sure?" I asked. "Yes, do it!" She writhed on the bed as I dragged my nails down the chalkboard.

Nina's primal scream filled the room.
She felt better. Two hours till Mark.
She could do this. She could figure out
how to cook something.

"Like a Sprite?" she said, knowing it was my favorite. "Yes." She put it on the bed just out of reach. I strained against the handcuffs.

Bert and Mary spiced things up, inviting Clara to join them for a threesome. Things went great till the nursing home staff walked in.

The leprechaun and I formed a partnership. He put up his pot of gold as collateral on my house loan, and I winged for him at the singles bar.

Karla snuck into my bed. "Oh, my God," she said, "you're wearing Spider-Man pajamas." She left, returning quickly dressed as Wonder Woman.

Kim was stunned to find Donna in bed with the goat. "How could you? I thought you loved me!" There was no response from the goat.

"You are my canvas," he whispered in her ear. "Paint me," she said. He dripped the colors across her body, putting the food to good use.

Joan just lay there, waiting for Bert to finish. It seemed to be taking a long time. How long could an 85-year-old millionaire live?

Afterward, Dylan laid his head on the pleasure-bot's chest. He tried not to cry. He had paid for sex, but what he needed was a cuddle.

"I like my sausages a little burnt," she said, cooking our breakfast. I felt a desperate urge to put my pants on.

I watched you run down the field with the ball, knowing you only did it for the money, never letting the public see your true passion, dance.

Tim nervously lay in bed with Trixy. The lamp gave off just enough light for him to read. "Warning, do not over inflate. Doll may pop."

I stabbed the pencil into the robot's eye and rolled over. The pleasure-bot had done its job, but I didn't want it watching me sleep.

Chocolate-covered strawberries. Soft music. Silk sheets. Darrin eased into the bed, hoping to get lucky on his third date with himself.

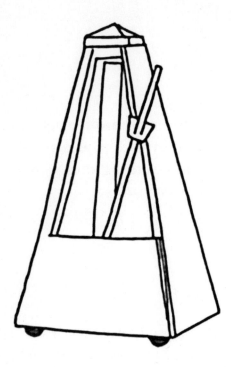

Kim moved perfectly in time with the metronome. Nick counted out the beats, helping her transform from music student to rhythmic lover.

Richard's park bench sat empty since his ascension. They wondered where he went, but no one was brave enough to sit there and find out.

"Margaret, what would you say if I spanked you?" "I don't know, sir." "Would you like it?" "Should I, sir?" "Yes." "Then I shall, sir."

Knight fought Dragon to win Princess's love. A mighty battle. The taste of victory! Princess lived happily ever after with Dragon.

Lovemaking with the mime was awkward. From what I could tell, she wanted me to pleasure her by riding a bicycle or hiding behind a wall.

"Spatula," said Rene. "Yes," said Ken. "Spatula, spatula, spatula," she said sexily. "Yes." "Toaster!" "Wait. Lost it. Go back to spatula."

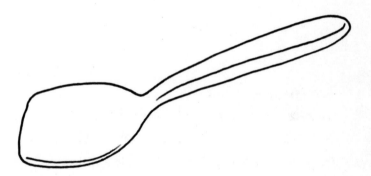

Chapter 5:

Work

Henry's first action as CEO was
to move all firings to Mondays. He
enjoyed them. Why delay the pleasure?

Stan dragged himself to the meeting,
sick from food poisoning. When asked
his opinion of the merger, he threw up
on the proposal.

The cougar paced the conference
room, a reminder that business was an
unpredictable animal that could eat you
at any time.

Phil looked out at John, gasping for air
on the moon's surface. He turned away.
Now, he would be captain, the position
he deserved.

Black car in front of the house. They found me. They'll try to take me back. I'll fight. The door opens. "Time to go, Mr. President."

"You want to hold hands?" said Bill. "Umm…OK," said Ken. They both needed a little comfort. It had been a tough staff meeting.

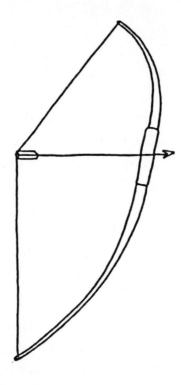

The arrow flew across the room and
pierced Justin's leg. His boss, Stuart,
reloaded his bow. Times were bad.
Everyone was downsizing.

"Will there be anything else, Mr. Landers?" Stuart paused. "You can bring me the staff report, Ms. Reed," he said, climbing off of her.

Ryan was confident his code was best. He didn't need feedback. Others should worship him. He would tell them if he ever saw anyone.

Paul was running out of options. The world was closing in. His survival instinct did the only thing it could, blame someone else.

Darla likes working. It's her best skill. When not working, she doesn't know what to do. To fill her free time she got a second job.

Carl was good at small things like buttering toast or stacking neatly. It was big things like talking to people that gave him trouble.

To cushion the blow, I gave out a cookie when I fired someone. It made them smile...until they realized it was stale...just like them.

I watched Monday crying in the corner, no longer the bully it once was, having lost its power over me now that I'd started working on Sunday.

The power went out. The elevator stopped. In the dark you told me your fears and cried. The next day you fired me to keep your secrets safe.

"Laramy! You're fired!" The best words I heard that summer. No more Burger Hut. On to bigger things. Now I work at Burger Chalet.

The desk knew my secrets, 30 years of
business dealings and a secretary or
two. Now I was retiring. I burned it to
guarantee its silence.

I stood outside your door waiting to recite my poem. I hoped it would reach the humanity inside you and keep you from firing me.

Chapter 6:

Death

Roses were Jen's favorite flowers. Mark used Jen's checkbook to buy a dozen red roses and placed them next to her, in the wet cement.

"Write a story about hope," said Paige, clutching tightly to the end of the rope. "Yes," I said, watching till she fell into the darkness.

Walter looked down at his funeral, surprised to see people there. They actually missed him. Wished he'd known before taking the pills.

One. Two. Three. Jump. Seems easy, but I'm still here on our ledge... hesitating. Maybe you are working late this time...and not out with him.

I held her pretty hand, intertwining my fingers with hers. Enjoying the moment, then putting it with the rest in the freezer.

Day 67. Food running out, not sure what to do. Bomb contaminated everything top side. How much more of me can I eat and still survive?

Mark applied sunscreen to Laura, trying to keep her from burning. The time would have been better spent putting out the fire on the boat.

"You haven't seen Mr. Potato Head in days?" "That's right, detective," said his wife. "You want to explain the tater tots in the oven?"

I took the gun from her lifeless hand, aimed, and pulled the trigger. I loved her. She deserved more than to be listed as a suicide.

Pete realized too late that Rita was the Skull Crusher Killer and he was her next victim. Her legs squeezed as his muffled screams grew silent.

Eric noticed he was holding his breath, which was working against trying to drown himself. Even at this, he was a failure.

I met Barb in a coffee shop, where she sat in the back reading palms. I held mine out. She gasped, sensing she'd be my next sacrifice.

The dissection didn't go as planned. Mary displayed the symptoms, but I could find no physical evidence of the devil inside her.

Gerald challenged me to fisticuffs and I accepted. The winner to get Mary. He approached, and I, not fully understanding the rules, shot him.

Jacques spent his life working with wood. No time for family. Now, on his death bed, his figurines gathered round to bid him farewell.

I opened the largest box first and found a coffin with my name on it. My children had learned to give practical gifts that people could use.

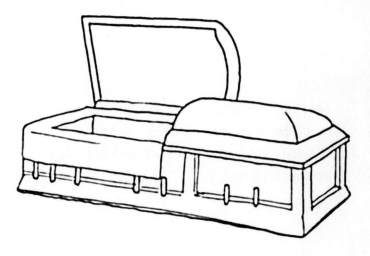

Derek was trapped at the very edge
of the cliff. The Russians drew their
knives. He hesitated, then leapt off,
betting on reincarnation.

Death gave Vicky a choice, heart attack
or childbirth. She chose childbirth,
but leaving her child behind broke her
heart anyway.

"Heads," said Jenny, watching the coin flip. "It's tails, you win," said John. Jenny reached over and pulled the plug on their mother.

First time I saw Rene, he said he would kill me. I thought he might. I was kissing his wife in bed. Funny how he ended up under my bus.

Voted out by the others, the goldfish floated to the top, an offering to the gods. The Great Paw took him to the beyond.

Today is special. Getting out of jail.
I will not go see Donna. I will not see
what shoes she's wearing. Too much
trouble to dig her up.

Marsha removed the corkscrew from
Dan. It was wrong to hurt others, but
he got what he deserved. He should
not have called her fat.

The helicopter lifted off. Mike looked down at Cindy, growing smaller as the fires closed in. Afraid of heights, she had stayed behind.

Each stroke of water heals my thoughts. I concentrate on being efficient, moving ahead. I try to not see her face as the boat went down.

The piano fell four stories, crushing Calvin. He had recently given up piano to study guitar. Upstairs, his teacher ordered a new piano.

Martha snuggled up to Rick. He smelled so good. So many questions she wanted to ask about his life. It made her wish he were still alive.

My time at the river did its trick. My spirit feels renewed. Ready to get back to work. New contract, two people to kill. Know one of 'em.

Dissatisfied with the automatic-submission system, I manually submitted you to the afterlife, ending your suffering and mine.

I enjoy my walks at twilight. It's my favorite time of day. The moments between light and dark, good and evil, boredom and victim.

The fan blew out the smoke. There was
Barb, empty packs all around. Most
smokers kill themselves slowly; she
had done it all at once.

Standing in front of you, I protected you from the gunman, but as the bullet approached, I saw it had your name on it, and stepped aside.

I filled the puppy with poison and took him to the nursing home. The terminally ill smiled and held him as he licked them to death.

I paid the fee and opened the door to my fantasy. There you were, alive again. I soaked in the 15 minutes I could afford from selling our house.

Chapter 7:

Other Worlds

They celebrated Earth Day each year, remembering the planet their parents spoke of, from a time before the evacuations to space.

Dear Roommate, You hurt my feelings. I don't judge what you eat. Please don't judge what I eat. Life is already hard being a zombie.

I clawed my way through Friday, determined to get to the weekend. At 5 o'clock, I ran out of work and straight into the bus Death was driving.

Angus stood outside his locked front door yelling, "I'm sorry I said you weren't real!" Through the window his clone flipped him off.

Craig reached for his pen but it wasn't there. He ran home holding his head, trying to keep the idea from seeping out.

I saw a shooting star and wished you'd come home to me. Then I realized your sun just burned out right before my eyes and you were gone.

Today is unlike any other. It's been declared the first time-travel-free day by the council. Today's events are happening as they should.

Your face looked familiar. I searched
my mind for your name but had to
settle for saying "Good morning" when
you awoke next to me in the bed.

It happened again. Now, I know it's me. My brother cut in line. I had a vicious thought. Suddenly he kind of sizzled and fell over.

I'd been living as Peter for years when I bumped into him. He was a mess, having no idea how to care for the female body I'd swapped him.

Her enormous ass called to him like flame to a moth. He reached out to touch it. In an instant he was gone, and her ass was a little bigger.

"I want you to love me," said Edith, looking into his eyes. The Devil hesitated, calculating how to come out ahead on this deal.

I planted the pretty flowers in memory of you, but they were ruined when your hand clawed up through the dirt.

Phil woke up on the floor next to the bed. Since the séance, his ex-wife's spirit had taken over the bed, mad he was dating her sister.

Could tell by the clouds I was back on Earth. Don't know what they did to me, feel different.

Perfect for each other, they lived a block apart, but would never meet. They lived in different worlds. His was Facebook, hers was Twitter.

I climbed from raindrop to raindrop, then entered the Cloud King's castle. "Enough," I said, ready to fight for control of the weather.

Mark's foot had swollen to twice its normal size. His health insurance company was sympathetic, they sent him larger shoes.

Wilfred crossbred canines with chickens, producing winged dogs. All the rage in LA…till a leash got tangled in a power line.

I opened the window and looked at the moon. Your body was still there. The cameras had seen me do it, but no one had jurisdiction to try me.

The TV learned to turn itself on. It watched the family in the room. They just sat there staring. The TV got bored and turned off forever.

Keith realized he couldn't feel his heartbeat. Concerned, he went to have it checked. The doctor cleared his memory banks and rebooted.

Mary had a thing for werewolves, but she liked them shaved. A combo of her love for the moon and her job as a dog groomer.

The coffee called to Alex from the kitchen. He obeyed, drinking his fifth cup. It was in control of the body now. There was no more Alex.

The garden gnomes waited for night, then entered the house, posing the humans in funny ways, calling them "cute," before returning outside.

Hard being a superhero. Not a lot of me time. Turn off my phone for five minutes and everyone starts dying.

Holding her umbrella, the wind swept Annie into the sky. Felt like she was flying. She let the umbrella go. Oops, it had the magic.

Phil wanted to be the perfect father. He bought Danielle a pony. She rode it on the first, third, and fifth weekends of the month.

Noticed her legs first. Strong and lean.
Long scar on the back of one. I took
my time approaching. Kissed her on
the nose. Great horse.

I am lonely. I make paper people out of
old newspapers. We sit and talk. We
start to bicker. They throw me out,
bundled by the curb.

After a few days, I got used to being a bird. No more job. No more putting up with people's crap. Now, they had to put up with mine.

Tim and the rocket lifted off, leaving Earth behind to pick up his mail-order bride. He paid extra to ensure their bodies were compatible.

"You're a cow," said Farmer. "I'm a dog," said Cow. "Prove it." He threw a ball. Cow fetched. "All right, you can sleep in the house."

Saw myself coming out of the pharmacy the other day. Wondered what I had. Some things better not to know. Better go back to my own time.

I am lying in the sun looking at the clouds. That puffy one looks like you. "Phil?" I say. No answer. I guess we're still not speaking.

Earl's feelings hurt when people called him "swine." They said it like a bad thing. Wasn't he the one who would provide bacon for them?

The therapy seemed to be working until I realized I was the patient, not the doctor. It got worse when I discovered I was just the chair.

Timmy used the magic set he got for Christmas to bring the family dog back to life. I paid the vet, again, to put him back to sleep.

The villagers poked me with sticks, keeping me awake. Unable to dream my escape, I was forced to endure their temporary victory in this world.

"You have such an intriguing mind and such interesting thoughts. I wonder where they come from," she said, holding my brain up to the light.

One time, long ago, when you weren't looking, I swapped souls with you. Now yours is dirtier than mine. I want to swap back. Hold still.

Desperate, I unplugged all the clocks in my house. With time stopped, I hid in today, safely away from your impending visit tomorrow.

I explained to the maid the handcuffs belonged to my five year old. When she handcuffed herself to my bed, I knew my Spanish was bad.

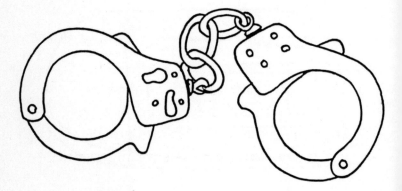

Rebecca reached into my dream and slayed the demons attacking me. I protected her in this world and she watched over me in all of the others.

I developed a drug that numbed the pain of being stuck in traffic, but something went wrong, and people started creating gridlock for pleasure.

Your eyes were a different color when we awoke. I knew you'd been replaced. Considered my options and played along. New you was good in bed.

About the Author

Sean Hill was overexposed to a potent combination of *Twilight Zone* and *Monty Python* as a child. This lead him down a dark path from which he has never fully recovered and bound him with a passion to storytelling.

Sean has spent much of his life combining creativity with work. Starting at age 19, he designed and programmed award-winning video games until he discovered improvisation, where ideas could be expressed as fast as they could be thought.

He is the Founder of the Hideout Theatre, the premier venue in Austin, Texas, for helping people expand their creativity through the study of improv comedy, storytelling, and the art of creating in the moment.

Using the skills he developed during 20 years of performing and teaching improv comedy, Sean has taught creativity, team building, innovation, and collaboration workshops to clients such as Motorola and the University of Texas MBA Program.

In 2009, Sean combined his love of writing and technology by creating @VeryShortStory, a Twitter feed where he interacts with his readers and creates 140-character stories.

When not writing fiction, Sean provides copywriting services and consults for clients who need to expand the creativity and collaboration skills of their staff.

Sean lives happily in Austin, Texas, with his wife, four children, and a lot of dogs. He can often be found performing improv comedy around town with his friends.

Contact Sean online:

E-mail: sean.hill@seanhill.com
Website: www.seanhill.com
Twitter: @sean_hill